God Is
with Me
through the
Night

written by **Julie Cantrell**

ZONDER**kidz**

ZONDERVAN.com/
AUTHOR**TRACKER**
follow your favorite authors

God Is with Me Through the Night
Copyright © 2009 by Julie Cantrell

Requests for information should be addressed to:
Zonderkidz, *Grand Rapids, Michigan 49530*

Library of Congress Cataloging-in-Publication Data

Cantrell, Julie, 1973-
    God is with me through the night / by Julie Cantrell.
        p. cm.
    Summary: A child is reassured by his mother that God loves him even when it is dark outside.
    ISBN-13: 978-0-310-71563-4 (hardcover)
    ISBN-10: 0-310-71563-6 (hardcover)
    [1. Christian life--Fiction. 2. Fear of the dark--Fiction.] I. Title.
PZ7.C173566Go 2009
[E]--dc22
{B}   2007022899

Published in association with the literary agency of WordServe Literary Group, LTD., 10152 S. Knoll Circle, Highlands Ranch, Colorado 80130

Zonderkidz is a trademark of Zondervan.

Design: Jody Langley

Photo Credits:
Page 11: Panthera Productions/Gallo Images/Getty Images
Page 17: Hiroyuki Ozaki/Amana Images/Getty Images
Page 18: John Guistina/Iconica/Getty Images
Page 19: Martin Ruegner/The Image Bank/Getty Images
Page 21: © Buyhotegg/Dreamstime.com
Page 29: Johan Elzenga/Stone/Getty Images

Printed in China

09 10 11 12 13 • 5 4 3 2 1

to Emily and Adam

At night I **play** with my family.

We laugh.

We snuggle.

I know I am not

alone.

But sometimes, after Mama
kisses me goodnight,

I start to feel **afraid**.

I hear **weird**
noises.

I see strange shadows.

Sometimes I Cry.

Mama tells me **God** is
with **me**, **even** in the **dark**.

Just like when God kept Daniel **safe** from the **lions,**

he will keep me **safe** too.

I say out loud,
"I am loved!"

I roar
like a
tiger,
"I am
safe!"

And then all the scary thoughts go away.
I fall asleep
and find my happy dreams.

I dream until morning,
 when all the darkness
is gone.

Then I wake up,
and I stretch.

I feel happy again.

In God's hands,
I am brave.

I am loved!

And I am safe.

"Do not fear,
for I am with you."

—Isaiah 41:10